The Clown Costume Mystery

By Eleanor Robins

Development: Kent Publishing Services, Inc.
Design and Production: Signature Design Group, Inc.
Illustrations: Jan Naimo Jones

SADDLEBACK EDUCATIONAL PUBLISHING
Three Watson
Irvine, CA 92618-2767

Website: www.sdlback.com

Copyright © 2006 by Saddleback Educational Publishing
All rights reserved. No part of this book may be reproduced
in any form or by any means, electronic or mechanical,
including photocopying, recording, or any information
storage and retrieval system, without the written permission
of the publisher.

ISBN-13: 978-1-59905-029-4
ISBN-10: 1-59905-029-3
e-book ISBN: 978-1-60291-458-2

Printed in China

13 12 11 10 09   4 5 6 7 8 9

Chapter 1

Steve was on the bus. The bus had just arrived at school. Steve got off the bus. Carl and Paige got off behind him.

All three were good friends. And they all lived at Grayson Apartments.

Steve said, "I need to go. See you both at lunch."

Carl said, "Good luck, Steve."

"Thanks. I will need it," Steve said.

"Why? Where are you going, Steve?" Paige asked.

"I'm going to Mrs. Drake's room," Steve said.

Mrs. Drake was an English teacher. She also helped with the drama club.

"Why are you going to her room now?" Paige asked.

"The members of the drama club are meeting there. We are going to find out who will be in the new play. I want to find out which part I got," Steve said.

"Do you still want the clown part?" Paige asked.

"Yeah," Steve said.

The play was about a clown. And the clown part was the best part.

"Do you think you will get the part?" Paige asked.

Steve said, "No. I think Kyle will get it. He is a good actor. He always gets the best part in all of the plays."

"Good luck. I hope you get it," Paige said.

"Thanks," Steve said.

"See you at lunch," Carl said.

Steve hurried into the school. And he went to Mrs. Drake's room.

Mrs. Drake said, "Hurry and get a seat, Steve. We don't have a lot of time. So we need to get started."

Steve was glad to see Brooke. So he quickly sat down next to her.

Steve liked Brooke. He wanted to date her. But she dated Dirk. Dirk was in Steve's math class.

Steve hoped Brooke and Dirk broke up. So maybe Brooke would date him.

Mrs. Drake said, "I will read all of your names. Then I will tell you which part you got. Some of you will have back-up parts."

Steve was sure that he got a back-up part, not a star part.

Mrs. Drake said, "Back-up parts are also big parts. You have to be ready to go on if someone isn't here. So study your part. And learn it well."

Steve could hardly wait to find out who got the clown part.

Mrs. Drake said, "Steve, you will be the clown."

Steve couldn't believe it. He got the part he wanted. And it was the best part in the play.

Mrs. Drake said, "That will mean a lot of work for you, Steve. But I am sure you can do it."

"Yes, I can do it," he said.

Then Mrs. Drake called Kyle's name. She said, "Kyle, you will be the back-up for Steve."

Steve wished he could see Kyle's face. But he couldn't see Kyle.

Mrs. Drake said, "Brooke, you will be the clown's wife."

Steve had hoped Brooke would be the clown's wife. And he knew that was the part she wanted.

Mrs. Drake told the rest of the students what their parts would be. Then she talked about how they could help with the play.

Then Mrs. Drake said, "Time to go. I will see you at rehearsal after school. Don't be late."

The students got up to go.

Kyle came over. He seemed mad.

Kyle said, "Mrs. Drake should have given that part to me, not you. I am the best actor. And you know that."

Steve said, "Yeah. You are the best actor. But Mrs. Drake thinks I am the best actor for this part."

"I don't think you are. And Mrs. Drake will find that out when we start

6

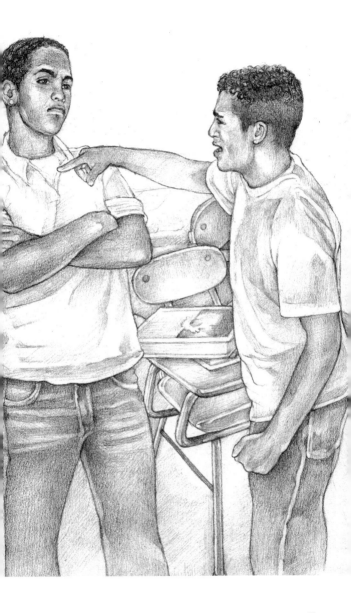

7

to practice. And then she will give the part to me," Kyle said.

"Don't count on it," Steve said.

Steve was going to work hard. He would show Kyle that he was the best one for the part, not Kyle.

Chapter 2

It was two weeks later. Steve was on his way to lunch. He had just heard some very good news. Brooke and Dirk had broken up.

Steve went into the lunchroom. He saw Carl. Carl was sitting at a table.

Steve got his tray. Then he went over to the table. And he sat down with Carl.

Steve said, "I just heard some good news."

"What?" Carl asked.

"You know I want to date Brooke. I just heard that she and Dirk broke up. So I am going to ask her for a date," Steve said.

"Are you sure that they broke up?" Carl asked.

"Three or four people told me they did," Steve said.

Carl said, "You better make sure before you ask Brooke for a date. You don't want to ask some other guy's girl for a date."

"OK. I will make sure before I ask her," Steve said.

He would ask Dirk and make sure. He didn't want to ask Brooke.

Paige came over to the table. Jack and Lin were with her. They sat down at the table.

Then Gail came over, too.

They were all good friends. Jack and Lin rode the bus with Steve, Carl, and Paige. Gail rode a special bus.

"Do you like the clown part, Steve?" Paige asked.

"Yeah," Steve said.

"Great news, Steve. I can't wait to see your play," Gail said.

"Me, too," Jack said.

"And me," Lin said.

Then all six started to talk about the new play.

They ate lunch. And they talked. Then lunch was over.

Steve put his tray away. Then he started walking to math class.

Steve saw Dirk. Dirk was walking down the hall in front of him. Dirk was on his way to math class, too.

Steve said, "Wait, Dirk. I will walk with you."

Steve wanted to ask Dirk about Brooke. He wanted to make sure they really had broken up.

Dirk stopped and waited for Steve.

Steve asked, "Did you and Brooke break up?"

11

Dirk seemed mad that Steve had asked him that.

"Yeah. I broke up with Brooke. Why do you want to know?" Dirk asked.

"I want to date her. Is that OK with you?" Steve said.

"Why should I care? I told you I broke up with her," Dirk said.

They got to math class. So the boys didn't say any more to each other. They hurried into the classroom. They were almost late.

Steve was glad Dirk broke up with Brooke. So it would be OK with Dirk for Steve to date her.

Steve worked hard in math class. But he was glad when class was over.

He hurried out to the hall. Dirk was right behind him.

Steve was looking for Brooke. And then he saw her. Steve hurried over to Brooke.

Steve said, "I heard you and Dirk broke up. How about going out on a date with me?"

"When?" Brooke asked.

"Friday night," Steve said.

"Sure. We can talk at rehearsal. But I have to get to class now, Steve," Brooke said.

"OK," Steve said.

Things were going really well for Steve. He had the best part in the play. And he had a date with Brooke.

Chapter 3

It was Monday morning. Steve was glad. He was ready for the week to start. The play would start on Friday. And he could hardly wait to play the clown.

Steve got to the bus stop. He was early. Only he and Carl were there.

Carl said, "I guess you are glad the play is this Friday."

"Yeah. I can hardly wait," Steve said.

"Your first play where you will be the star. How does it feel to be the star?" Carl asked.

"Great," Steve said.

Steve really was the star. So he didn't think Carl was joking with him.

"Is Kyle still mad because you got the clown part?" Carl asked.

"I don't think so. He was at first. But he doesn't seem like he is mad now. He just wants the play to be good. We need to sell many tickets. Then we can raise enough money to have another play," Steve said.

"I heard many people bought tickets," Carl said.

Steve said, "I heard that, too. I don't know if it is true. But I sold all of my tickets."

Carl laughed.

Then Carl said, "That doesn't surprise me. You made me buy one."

"I didn't make you buy one, Carl" Steve said.

"Just joking," Carl said.

And Steve was sure Carl was joking.

Steve said, "We have to turn in the money at rehearsal today. Mrs. Drake will tell us then how many tickets are left. So I can tell you tomorrow how many were sold."

The boys just stood there for a few minutes. And they didn't talk.

Then Carl asked, "How did your date with Brooke go?"

"Great," Steve said.

"What did you do?" Carl asked.

"We went to a movie. And then we got something to eat," Steve said.

"Did you and Brooke see Dirk?" Carl asked.

Steve said, "Yeah. He was at the movie. And then we saw him when we went out to eat."

"Did he have a date?" Carl asked.

"I don't know. I don't think so," Steve said.

"Did Dirk talk to you and Brooke?" Carl asked.

"No. But I don't think he saw us," Steve said.

"What are your plans? Are you going to go out with Brooke again?" Carl asked.

"Yeah. We want to go out again this weekend. But we can't. We will be too busy with the play," Steve said.

Some more kids came to the bus stop. So Steve and Carl didn't talk any more about the play or Steve's date.

Chapter 4

Steve was at rehearsal. The students had turned in their money.

Mrs. Drake said, "I can't believe it. You sold all of your tickets. And some of you want even more tickets to sell. We might have to give the play an extra day."

Kyle said, "Great. Then we can have another play soon."

Mrs. Drake said, "It is time for rehearsal to start."

Mrs. Drake put the money in a box. She left the box in the room next to the stage. The box didn't have a lock.

Then Mrs. Drake and the students went to the stage.

The students started to rehearse. They all wore their costumes. Steve wore his clown costume. He was the only one in a clown costume.

Mrs. Drake said, "You are doing a great job, Steve. Keep up the good work."

"Thanks, Mrs. Drake," Steve said.

Steve was on stage most of the time.

A few times Steve went out to get some water. And he had to go by the room where the money was kept.

The group practiced for a long time. But it didn't seem long to Steve.

Then Mrs. Drake said, "Time to stop for today."

Steve thought he did a good job. And Mrs. Drake said he did. Steve thought the others did a good job, too.

Mrs. Drake said, "All of you did a great job. See you tomorrow."

The students changed out of their costumes. Then they went home.

Steve wasn't at home long when the phone rang. It was Mrs. Drake.

"I need to see all of the drama club tomorrow. Come to my room before school. All of you have to be there," Mrs. Drake said.

"Is something wrong, Mrs. Drake?"

Mrs. Drake sounded very upset. Steve was sure something was very wrong.

"Someone took the ticket money during rehearsal. I found out after all of you left," Mrs. Drake said.

That surprised Steve very much.

"Who took the money, Mrs. Drake?" Steve asked.

Mrs. Drake said, "I don't know. I don't want to say this. But someone in the drama club must have taken it."

Steve said, "One of us? I don't believe that."

It couldn't have been one of them. They all cared too much about the play.

"Do you know who took the money?" Mrs. Drake asked.

"No," Steve said.

"Did you see someone near the money?" Mrs. Drake asked.

"No," Steve said.

"Did you go into the room where the money was?" Mrs. Drake asked.

"No," Steve said.

Why did Mrs. Drake ask him that?

"Are you sure?" Mrs. Drake asked.

Steve said, "Yes, Mrs. Drake. But why did you ask me if I am sure?"

At first Mrs. Drake didn't answer. But then she said, "Kyle saw someone in the room with the money. It was a person in a clown costume."

Steve was the only one who wore a clown costume. So Steve knew Mrs. Drake thought he had taken the money.

But how could Mrs. Drake believe he took the money?

"Kyle is wrong. I didn't go into the room with the money. And I didn't take the money," Steve said.

"Kyle didn't say you took the money. He saw someone in a clown costume. He didn't say it was you. But someone took the money," Mrs. Drake said.

"It wasn't me," Steve said.

"I didn't say it was you, Steve," Mrs. Drake said.

But Mrs. Drake sounded like she thought Steve took the money.

"I told Mr. Glenn the money was gone," Mrs. Drake said. Mr. Glenn was the principal.

"Mr. Glenn called the police. The police will be at the meeting tomorrow. And they want to talk to all of you," Mrs. Drake said.

Steve thought he knew what Kyle would tell them. Kyle would tell them about the person in the clown costume.

"Be sure you are at the meeting, Steve," Mrs. Drake said.

"I will be," Steve said.

Steve didn't want to go to the meeting. But he knew he would have to go. He had to find out who took the ticket money.

Chapter 5

Steve called Carl.

Carl said, "I thought you might call. Were many tickets sold?"

"Yeah. But I didn't call to tell you that. I need to talk to you, Jack, Gail, Lin, and Paige," Steve said.

"When do you want to talk to us? Before school tomorrow? Or at lunch?" Carl asked.

"Now. In front of my apartment," Steve said.

"Why now? What's wrong, Steve?" Carl asked.

"I am in big trouble. Really big trouble," Steve said.

"What kind of trouble?" Carl asked. He sounded worried about Steve.

"I will tell you when I see you. But hurry. I am going to call the others now," Steve said.

Carl said, "You call Jack and Gail. And I will tell Lin and Paige. We will meet in front of your apartment as soon as we can."

"Thanks," Steve said.

Steve called Jack and Gail. He told them he needed to talk to them now. And he asked them to meet him in front of his apartment.

Then Steve hurried outside.

It wasn't long until the other five friends arrived.

Carl said, "We are all here now, Steve. So tell us what is wrong. You don't look so good."

"That is for sure," Jack said.

"I am in big trouble. Really big trouble," Steve said.

"What kind of trouble, Steve?" Paige asked.

"Someone stole the ticket money. And Mrs. Drake thinks I took it."

"Why does she think that, Steve?" Lin asked.

"Kyle said he saw someone in a clown costume near the money. And I was the only one in a clown costume," Steve said.

"Were you near the money, Steve?" Carl asked.

"No. And I didn't take the money," Steve said.

"We know you didn't take the money," Paige said.

"Kyle didn't say I took it. He just said he saw someone in a clown costume near the money," Steve said.

"You were the only one in a clown costume. So it was the same thing," Carl said.

"Did someone else say they saw the person near the money?" Gail asked.

"I don't know. Mrs. Drake only said that Kyle did," Steve said.

"Maybe Kyle took the money. And he made up the story about the clown," Paige said.

"But why would he do that, Paige?" Steve asked.

"Maybe he said it so that you couldn't be in the play. And he could be the clown," Lin said.

"Yeah. So he could be the star. And not you," Carl said.

"Kyle took the money," Jack said.

"But it is OK with Kyle now. He was mad at first. But he isn't now," Steve said.

"Maybe he is still mad. And you don't know he is," Carl said.

"Kyle took the money. For sure," Jack said.

Gail said, "You don't know that, Jack. So don't say for sure that he did."

"But he could have taken the money," Carl said.

Jack said, "That is for sure. What can I do to help, Steve? Just say the word. And I will do it."

Paige asked, "Who is in the drama club? We can call them for you, Steve. And we can ask them if they saw someone near the money. Then we can meet back here in about 30 minutes. And we can share what we find out."

"Good idea, Paige," Gail said.

"That sounds like a plan to me," Carl said.

Steve said, "It feels good to know you believe me. And that you will all help me."

Steve felt a little better. Steve told his friends the names of the people in the drama club. Then they hurried off to call them.

Steve hoped his friends could find out something that would help him. They had to find out something. Or else he would be in big trouble. Not just with the school, but also with the police.

Chapter 6

Later that day, Steve was in front of his apartment. Four of his friends were with him. He could hardly wait to hear what they had found out. He hoped it was something that would help him.

Lin said, "Paige can't come, Steve. She has to help her mom. But she sent a message. She didn't find out anything that would help you."

"How about the rest of you? Did any of you find out where Kyle was? Could he have taken the ticket money?" Steve asked.

"He was with people the whole time. Three or four people told me that. So it couldn't have been him," Lin said.

"I heard the same," Jack said.

"So did I," Carl and Gail said.

"Did you find out anything that would help me?" Steve asked.

But Steve didn't think they did. They would have already told him if they had.

"No. Only bad news," Jack said.

"What?" Steve asked.

But Steve didn't want to hear more bad news. So he wasn't sure he wanted to know.

"Kyle wasn't the only one who saw the person in the clown costume near the money. Some others did, too. But they didn't tell Mrs. Drake," Carl said.

So Kyle didn't tell a lie just to get Steve in trouble.

"You are the only one with a clown costume. So they all think it was you," Jack said.

"But it wasn't me," Steve said.

"We know that," Gail said.

"Yeah. We do," Carl said.

But Steve knew that they were his friends. People who weren't his friends might not believe him.

"What am I going to do? I have to prove I didn't take the money. Or I will be in big trouble with the school. And with the police," Steve said.

"Don't worry, Steve. We are going to help you," Gail said.

"Yes. We will help you," Lin said.

Jack said, "What can I do to help?"

"Maybe you will find out something at the meeting tomorrow morning, Steve. Something that will help you," Lin said.

"Yeah. Maybe you will," Carl said.

But Steve didn't think he would.

Gail said, "We know Kyle didn't take the money. But maybe someone who was mad at you did. Can you think of someone who is mad at you?"

"No. Only someone who doesn't like me would do that. And I don't know anyone who doesn't like me. Do you?" Steve asked.

The other four looked down at the ground. No one said anything.

Steve said, "Don't all of you talk at the same time."

But no one talked.

"Someone answer my question. Do you know someone who doesn't like me?" Steve asked.

At first no one said anything.

Then Jack said, "Yes."

"Who?" Steve asked.

"Too many to name," Jack said.

That surprised Steve very much.

"That wasn't nice, Jack. You shouldn't have said that," Gail said.

Steve said, "You can't name even one person, Jack."

Or at least Steve hoped Jack couldn't do that.

"Dirk," Jack said.

"Dirk? Why wouldn't Dirk like me? I didn't do anything to him," Steve said.

"It is because of Brooke," Jack said.

"Why?" Steve asked.

"Because you had a date with her," Jack said.

Steve said, "Dirk and Brooke broke up. So why would he care if I date her?"

"He still likes her. And he wants them to get back together," Jack said.

Steve said, "I don't believe that. He was the one who broke up with her."

"But it is true," Jack said.

Steve looked at Carl.

Steve asked, "What about you, Carl? You know Dirk. Do you think that it is true?"

"Yeah. It is true. Dirk still likes Brooke. And he wants them to get back together. I thought you knew that," Carl said.

"I didn't. Is that why some other guys don't like me? Because I dated or tried to date their girls?" Steve asked.

"Yeah," Carl said.

"Maybe Dirk did take the money. Or maybe some other boy who doesn't like me took it. But how can I prove that?" Steve asked.

Chapter 7

For a few minutes his friends didn't answer. But they were all thinking about what they could do to help Steve.

Then Lin said, "I have an idea."

"What?" the other four asked at the same time.

"Where did Mrs. Drake get the clown costume, Steve? Do you know?" Lin asked.

"She got it at a store on Cramer Street," Steve said.

"Maybe someone else bought a costume like your costume," Lin said.

"And then wore it to steal the money," Carl said.

Lin said, "So this is my idea. We could go to the store. And we could talk to the owner. And maybe we will find out someone else bought a clown costume. One that is just like your costume, Steve."

"That sounds like a plan to me," Carl said.

Jack said, "Just say the word. And I will take you there."

Jack was the only one of them who had a car. So he was always glad to take them somewhere.

"Can you take us tomorrow after school, Jack?" Carl asked.

"Can do," Jack said.

"But that might be, too late, Jack," Steve said.

"Why?" Carl asked.

"The police will be at the meeting tomorrow morning. I need to find out something to help me before then," Steve said.

Gail said, "Maybe we can go now, Steve. Do you think the store is still open?"

Steve said, "Wait here. I will go inside. I will look up the phone number. Then I will call the store."

Carl said, "Good idea. Then we will know if it is open now."

Steve hurried inside. He looked up the number of the store. Then he called the store.

A man answered.

Steve was glad to know the store was still open.

Steve asked, "What time does the store close?"

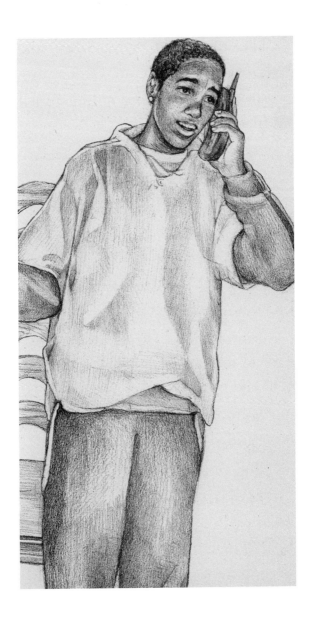

The man told Steve when the costume store closed.

Steve quickly hurried outside to tell his friends.

"What did you find out, Steve?" Carl asked.

"The store is still open. But only for an hour," Steve said.

Lin said, "Good. We still have time to go over there. And maybe we can find out something to help you, Steve."

"I think this is a good idea. But we have to tell our parents before we go," Gail said.

"Yeah. We had better do that, Gail," Steve said.

"But we need to hurry," Carl said.

"Meet back here in ten minutes. Then we can go. Is that OK with you, Jack?" Lin said.

"OK with me," Jack said.

"Thanks to all of you for the help," Steve said.

"Don't thank us yet, Steve. Wait until we find out who really took the money," Gail said.

"Right. Because we will find out," Carl said.

Steve hoped Carl was right. But he wasn't sure they would find out who took the money.

But they just had to find out who really took it. Or Steve would be in very big trouble.

Chapter 8

Steve went inside to tell his parents. Then he hurried back outside. He couldn't wait to go to the costume store.

Steve walked over to Jack's car. Jack sat in the car. Carl and Lin were standing next to it.

Gail wheeled up to them. She had their school yearbook. It was the one from last year.

Gail said, "My mom said I can't go. She said I need to study."

Gail handed the yearbook to Steve.

Gail said, "Take this with you. You might need to show the owner a picture of Dirk. Or a picture of someone else."

"Good idea. Thanks," Steve said.

"I am sorry I can't go with you," Gail said.

"That's OK, Gail. You brought the yearbook. And we didn't think about that. So you have been a big help," Steve said.

Gail said, "Let me know what you find out."

"We will," Lin said.

Then Steve, Carl, and Lin got into the car with Jack.

Jack said, "Just say the word. And we will be on our way."

"Go," Steve said.

They drove off.

It didn't take long to get to the costume store. But it seemed like a long time to Steve.

Soon, Jack parked his car.

Then Jack said, "I might have to move my car. So I will wait here."

"OK," Steve said.

Then Steve, Carl, and Lin went into the costume store. Lin had the yearbook with her.

A man came over to them. The man said, "My name is Mr. Chen. Can I help you find something?"

Lin said, "No. We are just looking right now."

Mr. Chen walked to the other side of the store.

Carl said, "Steve, you look for a clown costume like your costume. And then we will ask if someone bought a costume like that."

"OK," Steve said. Steve started to look at the costumes.

It didn't take Steve long to find one like his. He took it over to Mr. Chen.

Steve asked, "Did someone buy a clown costume like this?"

46

"Maybe in the last few days," Carl said.

Mr. Chen said, "Yes. A couple of days ago. A boy about your age bought it from me."

"Did he say why he wanted a costume just like this?" Carl asked.

Mr. Chen said, "Yes. He needed it for a play at the high school. He said he has a costume like this. But he got a lot of paint on it. And now it doesn't look good. So he wanted a new one. So it would look good for the play."

Carl said, "You were right, Lin."

Lin opened the yearbook. She turned to a page with a picture of Dirk. It had pictures of a lot of other students, too. She showed the yearbook to Mr. Chen.

Lin said, "Please look at this page. Do you see a picture of the boy?"

47

Mr. Chen looked at the pictures. Then he pointed to the picture of Dirk.

Mr. Chen said, "This is the boy."

"Are you sure?" Steve asked.

"Yes. I am sure. But why do you want to know?" Mr. Chen asked.

Steve said, "The boy got me into a lot of trouble. And now I will be able to get out of trouble. Thank you very much, Mr. Chen."

Steve wasn't the only one with a clown costume. Dirk had one, too. But Dirk didn't have a good reason to buy the costume. And Dirk had wanted one just like the one Steve had.

Now Steve wanted to go to the meeting tomorrow. And he could hardly wait to get there. He was sure everything would be OK now.